WITHDRAWN

Hassenfeld Library
University School of Nashville
2000 Edgehill Avenue
Nashville, TN 37212
www.usn.org

THE COLD WAR CHRONICLES

The Bay of Pigs and the Cuban Missile Crisis

Bethany Bryan

Cavendish Square

New York

Published in 2018 by Cavendish Square Publishing, LLC
243 5th Avenue, Suite 136, New York, NY 10016

Copyright © 2018 by Cavendish Square Publishing, LLC

First Edition

No part of this publication may be reproduced, stored in a retrieval system, or transmitted in any form or by any means—electronic, mechanical, photocopying, recording, or otherwise—without the prior permission of the copyright owner. Request for permission should be addressed to Permissions, Cavendish Square Publishing, 243 5th Avenue, Suite 136, New York, NY 10016. Tel (877) 980-4450; fax (877) 980-4454.

Website: cavendishsq.com

This publication represents the opinions and views of the author based on his or her personal experience, knowledge, and research. The information in this book serves as a general guide only. The author and publisher have used their best efforts in preparing this book and disclaim liability rising directly or indirectly from the use and application of this book.

CPSIA Compliance Information: Batch #CS17CSQ

All websites were available and accurate when this book was sent to press.

Names: Bryan, Bethany, author.
Title: The Bay of Pigs and the Cuban Missile Crisis / Bethany Bryan.
Description: New York : Cavendish Square Publishing, [2018] | Series: The Cold War chronicles | Includes bibliographical references and index.
Identifiers: LCCN 2016056236 (print) | LCCN 2016057361 (ebook) | ISBN 9781502628633 (library bound) | ISBN 9781502628640 (E-book)
Subjects: LCSH: Cuban Missile Crisis, 1962--Juvenile literature. | Cuba--History--Invasion, 1961--Juvenile literature.
Classification: LCC E841 .B785 2018 (print) | LCC E841 (ebook) | DDC 972.9106/4--dc23
LC record available at https://lccn.loc.gov/2016056236

Editorial Director: David McNamara
Editor: Jodyanne Benson
Copy Editor: Rebecca Rohan
Associate Art Director: Amy Greenan
Designer: Alan Sliwinski
Production Coordinator: Karol Szymczuk
Photo Research: J8 Media

The photographs in this book are used by permission and through the courtesy of: Cover, Carl Mydans/The LIFE Picture Collection/Getty Images; pp. 4, 46 Keystone- France/Gamma-Keystone/Getty Images; pp. 8, 53 Photo12/UIG/Getty Images; p. 10 Imagno/Hulton Archive/Getty Images; p. 15 Keystone/Hulton Archive/Getty Images; pp. 19, 23 AP Photo; p. 21 File: Marx7.jpg/Wikimedia Commons/Public Domain; pp. 28, 38, 44, 65 Bettmann/Getty Images; p. 30 United Press International/File: Kennedy Nixon Debate (1960).jpg /Wikimedia Commons/Public Domain; p. 32 User: Zleitzen, own work/File: BayofPigs.jpg/Wikimedia Commons/Public Domain; p. 34 Donald Uhrbrock/The LIFE Images Collection/Getty Images; p. 49 Universal History Archive/UIG/Getty Images; p. 59 AFP/Getty Images; p. 63 World History Archive/Alamy Stock Photo; p. 68 © Wally McNamee/Corbis/ Getty Images; p. 70 http://www.loc.gov/pictures/item/91792202/John Ward Dunsmore/File: Washington and Lafayette at Valley Forge.jpg/Wikimedia Commons/Public Domain; p. 74 Maurizio Gambarini/AFP/Getty Images; p. 75 Sovfoto/UIG via Getty Images; p. 80 eBay Item 262147225708/MGM/Clarence Bull/File: Hedy lamarr - 1940.jpg/Wikimedia Commons/Public Domain; p. 82 AP Photo/ Lee Jin-man; p. 84 Peter Turnley/Corbis/VCG/Getty Images; p. 89 ITAR-TASS/Getty Images; p. 91 Movie Poster Image Art/Getty Images; p. 93 Alexei Druzhinin\TASS/Getty Images; p. 94 Ibrahim Ebu Leys/Anadolu Agency/Getty Images; pp. 96-97 Rhone Wise/AFP/Getty Images.

Printed in the United States of America

CONTENTS

Introduction:
The President's Announcement 5

1 Mounting Tensions 11

2 The Bay of Pigs and the
Cuban Missile Crisis. 29

3 The Faces of the Cold War 49

4 Negotiation and Innovation 71

5 The Legacy of the Bay of Pigs
and the Cuban Missile Crisis. 85

Chronology 101

Glossary 103

Bibliography 106

Further Information 108

Index 110

About the Author 112

President Kennedy addressed the nation on the Cuban Missile Crisis on October 22, 1962.

INTRODUCTION

The President's Announcement

In October 1962, many Americans were focused on the World Series between the New York Yankees and the San Francisco Giants. Some were planning for Halloween, dancing the "Monster Mash" to the hit song that was at the top of the Billboard charts. Johnny Carson was the new host of *The Tonight Show*, bringing his own brand of comedy to the airwaves. It wasn't until President John F. Kennedy made an announcement on live television on October 22, that the nation understood that the United States was on the brink of nuclear war with the Soviet Union.

But there wasn't a single American who could have been surprised at this turn of events, as the United States and the Soviet Union had been engaged in a long-standing conflict, historically known as the **Cold War**, since the end of World War II. The Cold War was a conflict that did not involve active warfare. Instead, it was limited to extreme distrust and a lack of **diplomacy** between the United States and the Soviet Union. But even without bloodshed, the conflict was dangerous. Both nations struggled to be the dominant world power through developing technology, including nuclear weapons technology. The United States had effectively ended World War II by dropping atomic bombs on the Japanese cities of Hiroshima and Nagasaki. In the "nuclear age" that followed, other nations raced to keep up with weapons technology by developing nuclear weapons of their own, and the United States government viewed the USSR (Union of Soviet Socialist Republics) as its biggest threat in the nuclear arms race.

Because of the Cold War, nuclear war was on every American's mind by October 1962. People who feared for the lives of their families built bomb shelters in their backyards. Schoolchildren practiced for an attack with "duck and cover" drills under the watchful eye of teachers and school administrators. To this day, you might see the familiar symbol of three yellow triangles in and around older buildings, indicating that there is a **fallout shelter** on site. This fear of nuclear war had been building for years. In October 1962, President Kennedy's announcement showed the American people that their concerns were justified.

What the president had learned a few days before his official announcement to the nation was that his long-term fears had been realized; the United States finally had confirmation that the USSR had placed nuclear missiles in the Communist nation of Cuba, just 90 miles (145 kilometers) off the coast of Florida. But, the United States also had long been stockpiling nuclear weapons against the Soviet government and had, in 1961, deployed its own intermediate-range nuclear missiles into Italy and Turkey—two nations that lay adjacent to the USSR. From those locations, the deadly missiles could easily reach the cities of Moscow and Leningrad (now Saint Petersburg). In short, both nations were armed against the other with weapons that could cost millions of lives, and these weapons were within firing range.

Cuba had been a point of contention between the Union of Soviet Socialist Republics (USSR) and the United States for a few years by this point in time. In 1959, Fidel Castro of Cuba overthrew the military dictatorship of Fulgencio Batista in Cuba and established the first Communist government in the Western Hemisphere. **Communism** was still a fairly new concept for Americans in the 1960s, and many saw it as a threat to their own freedom. They had watched the Soviet Union slowly claim more and more of Eastern Europe. China had become a Communist nation in 1949. So the idea of Communism in the nation of Cuba hit a little too close to home for both the American people and their government. Additionally, Batista, despite being a ruthless dictator, had been an American ally. American companies had interests in Cuba, from cattle ranches and sugar plantations, to mines and utilities. Unlike Batista, Fidel Castro was unhappy with American dominance in Cuba and, since taking over as leader, had been working to decrease American influence on the island by nationalizing the sugar and mining industries. By 1961, the United States had ended diplomatic relations with Cuba and begun to explore ways to overthrow Castro and push back against Communism.

That year, President Kennedy authorized an invasion—a plan originated by Kennedy's predecessor, Dwight D. Eisenhower—by Cuban exiles to overthrow Fidel Castro.

Historically known as the Bay of Pigs invasion, the attempt was a failure, with troops surrendering in less than a day. This attempt to relieve Fidel Castro of his control of Cuba had only done more to solidify the relationship between the Soviet Union and Cuba, with the United States as their common enemy.

For thirteen days after the discovery of nuclear missiles in Cuba, the two nations, led by United States president Kennedy and Soviet **premier** Nikita Khrushchev, engaged in tense negotiations that, if they had broken down, could

The Bay of Pigs invasion was carried out by around 1,400 Cuban defectors who were trained specifically for this mission by the United States.

have destroyed the world as we know it. These thirteen days have come to be known, historically in the United States, as the Cuban Missile Crisis.

In the following pages, we're going to take a closer look, specifically, at two events: the Cuban Missile Crisis and the Bay of Pigs invasion. We'll look back at the Cold War as a whole and examine how the larger conflict affected American relations with Cuba in the 1960s. We'll talk about the key players involved in the Bay of Pigs invasion and some other, lesser-known attempts by the United States government to remove Fidel Castro from power. We'll talk, in detail, about John F. Kennedy, Nikita Khrushchev, Fidel Castro, and some of the other individuals who played a role in the peaceful resolution of the Cuban Missile Crisis. We'll talk about negotiation and diplomacy and its role in what many have called "the most dangerous event in human history." Finally, we'll discuss the continued legacy of the Cuban Missile Crisis, the Bay of Pigs invasion, and the Cold War as a whole and see how these events are still relevant to modern culture and continue to impact life in America in the twenty-first century.

Czar Nicholas II (shown here with his son Alexei) faced a great deal of controversy and criticism throughout his rule.

CHAPTER ONE

Mounting Tensions

The history of the Cold War is made up of a series of events that were set into motion long before World War II, long before Communism took hold of Eastern Europe, and long before nuclear missiles existed. One cannot look at the impact of the Cuban Missile Crisis or Bay of Pigs invasion without first looking at the Cold War. And one cannot look at the Cold War without talking about the state of Russia in the early twentieth century.

Russia at War

The Russian people were angry with Nicholas II, **czar** of the Russian empire. He had assumed power in 1894, and he was not experienced in governing a nation. He mistrusted the ministers whose job it was to advise him and often overruled them when making large decisions. He was often focused heavily on carrying on his legacy, rather than more pressing matters of government. His son and successor, Alexei

Nikolaevich, was ill with hemophilia, and the emperor was determined to find a cure.

Russia went to war with the Japanese in 1904 over dominance in Korea and Manchuria. In 1905, they surrendered. The defeat was devastating to the Russian economy and the military. Later that year, riots broke out in Russia. Some of the riots turned violent and deadly. The Russian **Revolution** of 1905 resulted in a shift in power, from a monarchy where the czar ruled completely to a constitutional monarchy, which included a parliament, called the Duma. But this did little to fix food shortages and civil unrest. People felt that poor leadership was to blame.

When Russia entered the First World War in 1914, it was still recovering from the Russo-Japanese War and the ongoing instability of the Russian government. Nicholas II was known for making rash decisions based on his own whims. He dissolved the Duma any time they opposed his will. In 1915, he took personal control of the Russian military when he saw it was not performing well. This meant he would be spending a significant amount of time away from the capital and his responsibilities to the Russian people. In his absence, his wife, Alexandra, handled the country's domestic policy, relying heavily on Grigori Rasputin, a power-hungry religious zealot, for advice. The country was in crisis: the government was weak, and the people were suffering. By 1916, over 1.7 million Russian soldiers had died in combat, and five million more had been wounded. These casualties were the most devastating loss to a nation during any war in human history up to that point.

The Bolsheviks, a group of leftist revolutionaries led by Vladimir Lenin, believed they had a solution to what ailed Russia, and that solution was socialism—the idea that a government should be ruled by workers, soldiers, and peasants, distributing wealth and supplies to everyone equally. This seemed like a strong idea to a lot of Russian citizens who had been facing food shortages repeatedly over the past several decades as the country recovered from wars and uprisings. Lenin was firmly opposed to Russian involvement in World War I, and in 1917, he led the Bolshevik revolt against czarist rule, with the help of a lot of Russian soldiers and peasants who had joined the cause. Under the strain of seeing more and more Russian soldiers leave their ranks every day to join the revolution, the Russian government, after years and years of existing in a weakened state, had no choice but to fold to the wishes of the revolutionaries. They were also forced to withdraw their involvement in World War I in order to concentrate on fighting back against revolutionaries at home.

Nicholas II, who was in Mogilev at the time, still trying to personally manage the Russian military, caught news of the uprising and tried to catch a train back to Petrograd. But the Duma, weary of the many times the czar had refused their advice or taken away their power whenever he disagreed with them, prevented him from boarding the train. The Duma set up a provisional government, and the czar, now powerless, had no choice but to abdicate his throne. Later that year, though, the Bolsheviks overthrew the provisional government, sending Russia into the throes of civil war. Since his abdication, Nicholas II and his family had remained under house arrest in the Ural Mountains. But the Bolsheviks could not allow the possibility of the czar returning to power, so the family was executed on the night of July 16, 1918. Their deaths ended three centuries of Romanov rule over Russia. It was a new world for the Russian people.

The USSR and the World

The USSR was formed officially in 1922 after several years of Vladimir Lenin unofficially serving as the head of the new government. But Lenin's rise to power was also fraught with resistance, both from anti-Soviet Russians and extremists within his own party. He survived a 1918 assassination attempt that had left him badly wounded, and his health never fully recovered. So when Lenin died suddenly in 1924, the government was left leaderless again, until Joseph Stalin officially came to power in the late 1920s.

Around the world, people were watching history unfold in the newly established USSR, and Americans did not trust this new type of government. They also did not trust Joseph Stalin, who famously ruled his people with an iron fist on a level that Lenin had not. Stalin encouraged the Soviet people to spy on each other. He allowed his own army of secret police to go into people's homes and arrest anyone who had spoken out against him publicly. He set up forced labor camps. Many people were simply executed. Stalin also imposed government control over farms and agriculture. Farmers who did not cooperate were killed. This led to widespread famine across the republic. The Soviet people were starving once again.

Hitler and World War II

By the late 1930s, another war was imminent in Europe. Nazi Germany was on the rise. At the head of the movement was Adolf Hitler, the leader of the Third Reich. Hitler believed that the German race was superior to all others, and he wanted that race to grow and expand outside of the limits of the German borders. In the mid-1930s, he was working to

The nonaggression pact between Germany and the Soviet Union was signed on August 23, 1939. Stalin is standing second from the left.

build arms in preparation for a war that he felt was necessary. By 1938, he sent troops to Austria. The next year, he annexed Czechoslovakia. Other countries across Europe were still left shaky by the First World War and were not eager for a confrontation with the führer.

In August 1939, Stalin signed the German-Soviet Nonaggression Pact with Hitler. Hitler wanted to invade Poland, but he couldn't if it meant confrontation with the USSR. An agreement with the Soviet Union would give Germany the support it needed to guarantee eventual control of Poland. In early September 1939, Germany invaded Poland. The governments of France and Great Britain knew at that point that they could no longer stand aside and allow Germany to take control of Europe, and both nations declared war on Germany. Later that September, the USSR would join the invasion of Poland, which fell quickly with Germany attacking from the west and the Soviet Union attacking from the east. An emboldened USSR went on to attack the Baltic States: Estonia, Latvia, and Lithuania. Then Stalin would move in on Finland. However, Adolf Hitler was not a man to be trusted. His ultimate goal was to invade the USSR, even though he had signed an agreement with Stalin, and over the course of time in 1941 and 1942, Hitler invaded the USSR.

The United States, meanwhile, had been watching from afar, not yet ready to join World War II. The Soviet occupation of Poland led United States president Franklin Delano Roosevelt to denounce the Soviet Union as a dictatorship and a threat. But Roosevelt understood that Nazi Germany was the larger threat, especially after Germany

Stalin's Legacy

Joseph Stalin died on March 5, 1953. During his reign, he had worked hard to create a legacy of his own design, ordering history books to be rewritten to give him a greater role in the Russian Revolution. He changed the name of the city of Leningrad to Stalingrad. He had paintings made of himself, and he even added his own name to the Soviet national anthem. His final act in establishing his great legacy was to have his body placed beside Vladimir Lenin's body in his mausoleum in Red Square in the heart of Moscow. Lenin had ordered his own body to be preserved and kept on display. Stalin longed for the same, so when he died, his body was embalmed and placed beside Lenin's.

However, Stalin was responsible for the deaths of over twenty million people during his twenty-four years as the Soviet dictator, and not everyone was interested in having his body lie in a place of honor beside Lenin's. When Nikita Khrushchev assumed the role of premier of the USSR in 1957, one of his first goals was to "de-Stalinize" the USSR. In 1961, Stalin's body disappeared one night and was quietly buried elsewhere.

But Stalin's "cult of personality" continues to live on in Russia. New textbooks that were printed in Russia in 2007 praised Stalin's efforts to industrialize the USSR during his time as its leader. Polls conducted in 2008 showed that his popularity was on the rise again. Stalin represents a memory of Communist rule in Russia, and he continues to have supporters.

invaded the USSR. So when the United States finally joined the Allied forces after the attack on Pearl Harbor by Japan, they would fight alongside the Soviet Union, along with Great Britain, China, France, Australia, Belgium, Brazil, Canada, Denmark, Greece, the Netherlands, New Zealand, Norway, Poland, South Africa, and Yugoslavia, and several others as well. Even fighting side by side, however, the United States and the Soviet Union still had a relationship ruled by distrust.

By May, 1945, Harry S. Truman had been sworn in as president of the United States following the death of Franklin Roosevelt a month before. The global conflict had all but ended in Europe, following the defeat of Germany and the suicide of Adolf Hitler. But fighting continued to rage in the Pacific, so the United States sought to end World War II by dropping the first deployed atomic bomb over the Japanese city of Hiroshima. Three days later, the United States government dropped a second bomb on the Japanese city of Nagasaki. Japan surrendered, effectively ending the war that was still raging in the Pacific and ultimately World War II.

The Cold War Conflict

Writer George Orwell, author of *Animal Farm*, was the first to coin the term "cold war" to describe a conflict where no blood was shed. Although the Soviet Union and the United States were not engaged in active military combat and had been allies during World War II, they were decidedly locked in conflict. The USSR was slowly expanding into

Eastern Europe, worrying many Americans about the spread of Communist ideals globally. The Soviet people resented American involvement in foreign conflict. Hostility grew on both sides.

Owning your own fallout shelter was all the rage in the United States during the Cold War.

Mounting Tensions 19

As a result of this fear, the United States government adopted a "containment" strategy against the USSR, where they would maintain a "firm and vigilant" strategy that kept the USSR from further expansion, basically by providing assistance to countries where this expansion was in process.

The Nuclear Arms Race

When the United States dropped the two atomic bombs that ended World War II, other nations clamored to arm themselves with nuclear weapons of their own. The Soviets tested their first atom bomb in 1949. As a result, President Truman announced that the United States would create a weapon with even more destructive potential. They called it the "Super Bomb," a hydrogen bomb with massive destructive potential. The USSR followed suit and developed a hydrogen bomb in 1953. The threat of nuclear attack affected Americans on a very personal level. People built bomb shelters in their backyards and schools, and other public places began running drills so that everyone would be ready in case of an attack. Americans began to live in a constant state of fear.

The Fear of Communism

The Communist ideology that was later adopted by Russia in order to found a new form of government after the Russian Revolution was born from *The Communist Manifesto*, a pamphlet written by Karl Marx and Friedrich Engels in the mid-nineteenth century. The kind of Communism outlined in the pamphlet called for an end to the class system. The working class would rise up and rule. Goods would be shared equally among the people. And, with any luck,

Karl Marx was one of the two authors—Friedrich Engels was the other—of *The Communist Manifesto*, a pamphlet that laid out the idea of a socialist society.

the Communist ideology would go global, taking down capitalism and ridding the world of the wealthy upper class for good.

The United States was built upon a capitalist system of government, and while many Americans could see and understand the benefits of a Communist society, they were not eager for their own government to face the kind of upheaval that had occurred in Russia in the early twentieth century. But socialism was taking over the world. The USSR had been formed in 1922, the first nation to be governed under Communist rule. China followed suit in 1949, creating the People's Republic of China. By 1950, almost half of the world's population lived under Communist rule, so tension surrounding the possible existence of Communism in the United States, particularly within the government, was an enormous concern. Many Americans were worried about "reds" taking over their country. Politicians running for office had to take a firm stand against Communism if they wanted to win elections. Free speech and basic civil liberties, both guaranteed by the United States Constitution, began to fall to the wayside.

Cuba on the Rise

The fear of Communism among Americans had been prevalent since before World War II began. Until the late 1950s, however, Communism had remained safely on the other side of the globe. But then Fidel Castro arrived back in Cuba with a renewed sense of purpose and an army of followers.

FIDEL CASTRO RUZ

The future dictator of Cuba, Fidel Castro, is shown here as a young man.

Fidel Castro was a tireless force of change in Cuba and had been fighting the tyrannical rule of dictator Fulgencio Batista since 1952. But while Batista welcomed trade and commerce with the United States, Castro did not. So when Castro took over as prime minister of Cuba in 1959, it sent the United States into an uproar. Cuba is only about one

Joseph McCarthy Takes on Communism

With World War II still heavy on the minds and consciences of the American people, Joseph McCarthy, a former marine, was elected to the United States Senate in 1946. A conservative leader, McCarthy kept a low profile through his first term in office, working on housing legislation and sugar rationing. But with his second term looming in 1950, McCarthy needed a platform that would hand him a win, and fast. On February 9, 1950, the senator went public with the claim that he had a list of over two hundred individuals in the State Department who were members of the American Communist Party. This revelation confirmed many Americans' worst fears—that Communism existed right there in America. Suspicion loomed, and many called for an investigation. McCarthy was, of course, happy to lead the charge against those on his "list."

There was only one problem. While there were many actual Communists on McCarthy's list (a few were, in fact, spies working for the Soviet Union), there were others who were simply left-leaning politicians who disagreed with McCarthy's political views. But despite these findings, McCarthy pushed onward, becoming chairman of the Government Committee on Operations of the Senate and working to root out Communists in government. However, much of McCarthy's "evidence" was without merit, and those who spoke out against McCarthy were soon investigated for ties to Communism as well. Over two thousand government employees lost their jobs because of McCarthy's investigations. Some suffered long-term effects, shunned in their homes and communities and unable to find work.

Finally, in 1954, McCarthy turned his attention to investigating Communist infiltration of the United States Army. Some who had originally supported McCarthy began to call his actions into question. President Eisenhower, while never speaking out publicly against McCarthy, quietly went about shutting down the McCarthy's investigations. In 1954, the hearings were brought to an end, but McCarthy remained in office. The so-called "red scare" was over. McCarthy was soon diagnosed with cirrhosis of the liver and died in 1957 at the age of forty-eight.

hundred miles (161 km) from Florida, and it was the first Communist nation in the Western Hemisphere. (Castro publicly denied being a Communist until 1961, but he set to work nationalizing a lot of businesses in Cuba, which is an act of Communism.) Communism suddenly felt closer than ever to the American people. More importantly, it was a little too close for the comfort of the American government. Cuba was just one country, but several countries in Latin America were ruled by dictatorships in the late 1950s and early 1960s. If Communism could rise in Cuba, where would it go next? Where would it end?

The Trade Embargo

One of Fidel Castro's first acts as the new leader of Cuba was to nationalize businesses that represented American interest in Cuba. Mining companies, factories, and plantations were taken over by the Cuban government without any kind of compensation being paid to the company owners. Castro increased taxes on United States imports. When the United States responded by limiting trade with Cuba and imposing the first trade **embargo** in 1960, Castro decided to negotiate for necessary goods with the Soviet Union instead. In 1962, President Kennedy expanded the embargo and made it permanent, effectively cutting off diplomatic relations between Cuba and the United States. (The embargo remains in place to this day, but relations between the United States and Cuba are slowly improving.)

Cuba and the Soviet Union

As diplomacy between the United States and Cuba began to fall apart, the relationship between the Soviet Union and Cuba grew. Cuba began to rely on the USSR for trade and military support. This was not good news for the United States, for two enemy nations to join forces. But a relationship between the Soviet Union and Cuba was mutually beneficial. The Soviet Union would supply oil, food supplies, chemicals, and other vital materials, and Cuba would sell the USSR its sugar. This would also provide the Soviet Union with an ally that was close in proximity to the United States. If the Cold War conflict was to come to a head, this was its moment to do so.

ERECTOR ON

OXIDIZER VEHICLES

PROB HYDROGEN PEROXIDE TANKS

MISSILE READY BLDGS

FU

ERECTOR ON LAUNCH PAD

MISSILE ON TRAILER

This is one of the images shown to President John F. Kennedy as evidence that Cuba was in possession of nuclear missiles.

CHAPTER TWO

The Bay of Pigs and the Cuban Missile Crisis

Cold War tensions dominated the 1960 presidential campaign between then-Vice President Richard Nixon and Senator John F. Kennedy. Kennedy was young, and questions arose about the political experience of someone his age. Nixon had the support of sitting president Dwight D. Eisenhower. It looked like his experience and the support of the Republican Party would take him straight to the presidency.

Some historians say that it was actually Kennedy's youth and charisma that got him elected. Eighty-eight percent of American households had televisions by 1960. For the first time, they were able to tune in to watch the presidential debates. During the first debate, Kennedy was poised and oozed charisma. He spoke directly to the cameras and the American public watching at home. Nixon spoke to his opponent, as was standard in debates before the medium of television. Almost immediately following that first debate, the question of Kennedy's experience faded away. The

The presidential debates between Richard Nixon and John F. Kennedy were the first to be televised across the United States.

United States would go on to elect John F. Kennedy, the president who would lead the nation through one of the most dangerous confrontations of the Cold War.

The Bay of Pigs Invasion

The United States was in a state of desperation over Cuba. Fidel Castro was working hard to establish Communism in Cuba by ridding the country of American influence, and this was helping to build a strong relationship with the USSR. The country needed to act, and quickly.

President Eisenhower had been in the process of forming a plan when his term ended, so when President Kennedy took office in 1960, the Bay of Pigs invasion was already set in motion. (It was not known by this name at the time.) The plan was this: the United States would train an army of

Cuban exiles, known as Brigade 2506, and give them all the supplies they needed. Then, those exiles, led by José Miró Cardona, a former member of Castro's government and head of the Cuban Revolutionary Council, would invade Cuba and perform a series of aggressive tactics in an attempt to weaken Castro's forces. There would be two air strikes against Cuban air bases to destroy Castro's air force and prevent him from retaliating. Once that was complete, a ground force would move in, aided by paratroopers dropped in before the invasion. The Cuban people and military forces that opposed Castro, seeing that help was arriving, would then rise up and try to help take back the government. If the plan was successful, Cardona would then be in the perfect position to take control of the Cuban government as its provisional president, creating a pro-American Cuban government once again. But, according to the CIA, the fact that the United States was involved had to remain a secret because if the Soviet government found out, they might retaliate, leading to that escalation of the Cold War that had been on American minds for almost two decades.

Originally, the land invasion by Brigade 2506 was set for the anti-Castro community of Trinidad, where a lot of revolutionary groups had set up shop. But when Kennedy's concerns over keeping the American involvement secret grew, he asked that the CIA come up with a different location. This is when the Bay of Pigs was chosen as the landing point for the attack. The area was swampy. Forces would likely not run into any resistance. A small force would also invade on the east coast of Cuba as a distraction. The stage was set.

Where It All Went Wrong

The Bay of Pigs invasion was a disaster from the start. The first issue was that the Bay of Pigs itself was a terrible location for an invasion. The Escambray Mountains served as the escape site for the invaders in case anything went wrong, but to get to the mountains from the Bay of Pigs, the forces would have to cross around fifty miles (80 km) of hostile territory. And if the United States and the Cuban **guerrilla** force wanted to create an uprising, a swamp where hardly any anti-Castro revolutionaries lived was not a good location for it.

This map of Cuba shows the location of the Bay of Pigs, which turned out to be a poor location for an invasion.

On April 15, 1961, six bombers left Nicaragua to initiate the first of the two air strikes against Cuba's air bases. The CIA had used World War II B-26 bombers that they had refurbished and painted to look like Cuban air force planes, with the idea that it would look like the Cuban pilots simply "defected" and bombed their own air force base as an act of resistance. But the bombers ended up missing a lot of their targets. At the end of the first air strike, much of Castro's air force was still in working order. News of the attack became public, and so did photographs of the repainted bombers.

At an emergency session of the United Nation's Political and Security Committee, United States ambassador to the United Nations Adlai Stevenson adamantly denied American involvement in the invasion because he had not been told about the operation. President Kennedy had to make a fast decision. He could admit to American involvement in the air strike or deny it and allow the plan to continue. He knew that he couldn't lie to the United Nations because it would create bad relations between the United States and the rest of the world. President Kennedy quickly cancelled the second air strike.

This change in plans didn't mean that the invasion was over, however. The land invasion was still on, as planned. However, Brigade 2506 ran into unforeseen challenges as well on the morning of April 17. The Bay of Pigs was filled with coral reefs, making it difficult for them to reach the shore. Many of the invading forces lost a good deal of equipment and weapons to the waters of the bay. When the brigade landed, the Cuban government already knew what was coming, and the invaders came under fire by those Cuban air force planes that hadn't been destroyed two days before. Castro sent around twenty thousand troops to the Bay of Pigs, which meant that Brigade 2506 was vastly outnumbered.

One set of paratroopers who were meant to drop in to provide support missed their target and then lost most of their equipment to the swamps, leaving them unable to help.

James Donovan: Negotiator

The movie *Bridge of Spies* tells the true **espionage** story of a Brooklyn lawyer who was asked to defend a Russian spy and eventually negotiate his return to the Soviet Union, in exchange for the lives of two Americans that were being held by the Soviets. The lawyer, James Donovan, had experience in this type of thing, as he had been associate prosecutor at the Nuremberg Trials—trials at which twenty-two major Nazi war criminals

James Donovan was a lawyer and US Navy officer, but he was best known for his role as an international diplomatic negotiator.

were tried for the atrocities they committed during the Holocaust. After ten days of negotiating with Soviet mediators in East Germany, the exchange occurred, and Donovan returned to the United States.

When the United States government came to James Donovan in need of his help again, this time he would be negotiating for the lives of over a thousand prisoners: the members of Brigade 2506, captured after the failure of the Bay of Pigs invasion.

Donovan was good at what he did. He traveled to Havana several times to meet personally with Castro. He worked hard to gain Castro's trust, and he was careful to never interrupt Castro or try to speak over him. Donovan brought his eighteen-year-old son with him to show that he trusted Castro. Castro was impressed by this gesture and took Donovan fishing—in the Bay of Pigs, his favorite spot. The negotiations grew tense during the Cuban Missile Crisis, and Donovan was forced to temporarily put an end to his visits to Cuba. But with the Cuban Missile Crisis behind them, he went right back.

In the end, it was a matter of trying to figure out what Cuba needed and what they would be willing to accept in exchange for the lives of 1,113 prisoners. The answer was simple: food and medicine. In the end, the United States delivered fifty-three million dollars in food and medicine, and Castro released the members of Brigade 2506. But Donovan wasn't done. He went on to negotiate for the release of ten thousand political prisoners who were being held in Cuban prisons—by July 1963.

Another group of paratroopers managed to interrupt road travel and held back some of the Cuban forces, but as the rest of the plan fell apart, so did their blockade.

The United States worked to send aid and rescue to the brigade. President Kennedy authorized six American fighter jets to help defend the brigade's aircraft as they flew in to help, but the jets arrived too late. The report on the Bay of Pigs on the CIA website tells the story that the fighter jets left an hour late because of a miscommunication. The story from Kennedy's Presidential Library and Museum says that the time change between Nicaragua and Cuba was the culprit. Either way, the unguarded brigade aircraft contributed to the killing of over one hundred members of Brigade 2506. Another twelve hundred finally surrendered and were sent to Cuban prisons.

Castro's Perspective on the Bay of Pigs

Fidel Castro knew all about the Bay of Pigs, the bay itself, and also the invasion that was headed his way. Castro took frequent vacations to the Bay of Pigs, fished there, and invested in the peasants who lived in that area. Because of this, Cubans who lived in the area surrounding the Bay of Pigs liked their leader. Castro knew about the invasion because Cuban exiles living in Miami had caught wind of the plan. It was common knowledge. And Cuban intelligence alerted Castro to the guerrilla training camps in late 1960 before Kennedy was even inaugurated in February 1961. So while Castro didn't have all of the details, he knew something was coming, and he had a pretty good idea that the United States was behind it.

Before the first air strike began, some sources say that Castro moved a good majority of his air force out of harm's way. He was also prepared for an uprising by the Cuban people. He gathered potential dissidents together in theaters, military bases, and stadiums. He kept them there, unable to join the invading forces.

During the land invasion by Brigade 2506, Castro set to work sinking the invading ships carrying troops and supplies. The USS *Houston* was severely damaged, and its captain was forced to beach it in the bay. The USS *Rio Escondido*, loaded with fuel, was hit by machine-gun fire before it exploded and then sank.

Fidel Castro had the upper hand in this battle, and he knew it. For him, it was simply a matter of waiting for surrender.

Bobby Kennedy and Operation Mongoose

Politically, the Bay of Pigs invasion was a catastrophic failure for the Kennedy administration. Kennedy was a young president, and early in his administration, he was still working to prove that he was an effective leader. General Maxwell Taylor, a retired United States general who had led an investigation into the Bay of Pigs incident finally delivered the report of his findings: "There can be no long-term living with Castro," the report read. Kennedy needed to keep working to loosen Castro's grip on Cuba. He could not back down.

At this point, the president needed someone he could rely on absolutely to see a plan through. He, of course, called on his most trusted ally: his younger brother, Bobby Kennedy. The simplest solution to their problem was to take out Castro once and for all. The plan was called "Operation Mongoose." The mongoose, as it exists in nature, is a predator, primarily found in Africa. It is known for fearlessly attacking venomous snakes, like cobras. That is exactly what the United States government would do—operate like a mongoose and kill the snake, Fidel Castro.

Robert F. Kennedy was John F. Kennedy's younger brother and acted as attorney general and his brother's closest advisor during JFK's presidency.

The Bay of Pigs invasion was a large-scale operation. Operation Mongoose would be a small, covert one. Bobby Kennedy brought in CIA operative Edward Lansdale, who had famously fought Communists in the Philippines, an act that possibly inspired a character in Graham Greene's novel *The Quiet American*. Lansdale took charge of Operation Mongoose, coordinating the plans with the CIA and the Department of Defense. The plan was not a simple one. It consisted of multiple operations that would ultimately lead to the assassination of Fidel Castro. This was meant to take place in October 1962. But, for whatever reason, the plan did not move forward. Ultimately, President Kennedy called off Operation Mongoose in order to focus on a larger situation that was brewing: there was proof that the Soviets had placed nuclear missiles in Cuba.

The Cuban Missile Crisis

Arthur C. Lundahl had a unique job. He was the CIA's chief photo interpreter. The photographs that he would present to President Kennedy and the members of his cabinet on October 16, 1962, were grainy. To the untrained eye, they might look like a blurry image of fields and a few winding roads. President Kennedy himself remarked that what was shown in those images could have been mistaken for a football field. But Lundahl had labeled the photos, and there could be no mistaking what was really in the photographs: erector launcher equipment and missile trailers. The Soviet government was constructing nuclear missile bases in Cuba, from which an armed missile could reach

New York Times, October 23, 1962

The Internet gives us news with the push of a button, but during the Cuban Missile Crisis, Americans had to rely on print journalism to keep up with the latest from the White House. The headline on the *New York Times* the day after Kennedy made his televised announcement to the word read: "U.S. Imposes Arms Blockade on Cuba on Finding Offensive Missile Sites; Kennedy Ready for Soviet Showdown."

It should be noted that during his speech, Kennedy placed the blame firmly on the Soviet government, according to the *New York Times* article that reported the story: "Two aspects of the speech were notable. One was its direct thrust at the Soviet Union as the party responsible for the crisis. Mr. Kennedy treated Cuba and the Government of Premier Fidel Castro as a mere pawn in Moscow's hands and drew the issue as one with the Soviet Government."

The other aspect of Kennedy's speech that the *New York Times* pointed out was that the United States would stay firm on handling the threat alone: "The other aspect of the speech particularly noted by observers here was its flat commitment by the United States to act alone against the missile threat in Cuba."

The article also emphasized the fact that Kennedy would work hard against the threat, even if opposed by United States allies: "But the President emphasized that discussion in any of these forums would be undertaken 'without limiting our freedom of action.' This meant that the United States was determined on this course no matter what any international organization—or even the United States' allies—might say."

You can read more of the *New York Times* report on the Cuban Missile Crisis in the newspaper's archives.

almost any location on the East Coast. A nuclear missile launched from the missile site could reach Washington, DC, within thirteen minutes.

The United States needed to act quickly. President Kennedy created a special Security Council to help him manage the crisis, called the Executive Committee (EXCOMM). Because Kennedy was not ready to go public with the news that the nation was in harm's way and set off a national panic, he had to continue to perform his job normally, while secretly meeting with EXCOMM. On October 20, it was decided that the best solution was firm diplomacy, rather than aggression.

The United States would place a blockade, made up of American ships, around Cuba to keep Soviet supplies from entering. With that in place, the president would demand that the missiles be removed from Cuba by a certain deadline.

Nikita Khrushchev's Perspective

The only problem with the blockade strategy was that the United States had missiles of its own, in Turkey and Italy, and Nikita Khrushchev knew all about them. So putting missiles in Cuba was partially a defense strategy against the United States. Khrushchev couldn't very well remove missiles from Cuba and leave his own nation and its ally—Cuba—defenseless.

Furthermore, Cuba and the Soviet Union had taken the Bay of Pigs invasion as an act of American unprovoked aggression. The USSR had stayed out of the conflict, but Khrushchev felt that Cuba needed Soviet protection even if it meant not disclosing this information to the United States government.

In a 2012 interview with the United States Naval Institute (USNI), Khrushchev's son Sergei said that the United States was simply not used to having to deal with threats at such close proximity. He said, "Americans were lucky. They lived all the time protected by two oceans. So they're scared at everything as a nation. I would compare Americans to a tiger that grew up in the zoo and then was sent into the jungle."

Kennedy Addresses the Nation

On October 22, President Kennedy spoke to the nation in a televised address. He announced that a number of measures would be taken in order to protect the United States at all costs. For six days after Kennedy addressed the nation, the United States and the Soviet Union entered into tense negotiations. Around the nation, people set to work replenishing supplies in their backyard bomb shelters. Other Americans sent telegrams to Washington, begging for leaders to solve the crisis. Some took to the streets in protest. Was it right for the president to set up the blockade around Cuba, or would that escalate the problem? Other protestors pushed for war with the Soviet Union. Business owners who profited from weapons manufacture looked forward to the lift in the economy they had experienced during World War II. Around the nation, American citizens had mixed feelings about the situation going on in Cuba.

On the eighth day of the Cuban Missile Crisis, October 23, 1962, the ships sent by the United States to quarantine Cuba moved into place, cutting off supplies to Cuba from the Soviet Union.

Nikita Khrushchev's Perspective

Khrushchev and the Soviet Union did not take the American quarantine of Cuba as simply a quarantine. They saw it as a threat and an act of intimidation—even as an act of piracy. In a letter to the United States president on October 24, he said, "You, Mr. President, are not declaring a quarantine, but rather are setting forth an ultimatum and threatening that if we do not give in to your demands you will use force. ... You are no longer appealing to reason, but wish to intimidate us."

Khrushchev knew, however, that he needed to be cautious. He didn't want a confrontation with American forces. Therefore, he ordered most of the ships that were en route to Cuba to return to the Soviet Union. Nonmilitary ships, such the oil tanker *Bucharest*, however, could continue on to Cuba. He conveyed this information in a message to President Kennedy. He sent a separate message to Fidel Castro denouncing the aggressive actions of the United States and asking for Soviet troops in Cuba to be on high military alert.

Castro's Perspective

Castro told his aides that it looked like war was imminent between the United States and the Soviet Union. Truth be told, the Cuban leader felt that Khrushchev was not being firm enough in dealing with demands from the United States. Was Khrushchev correct to return missile-carrying Soviet ships to the USSR, or did it make them look weak?

Castro also saw signs of the United States trying to drive a wedge into Cuba's alliance with the Soviet Union. Castro's

Fidel Castro, standing second from the right among his compatriots, led the revolution that would unseat Cuban president Fulgencio Batista from power.

brother Raul and Che Guevara were both out of Havana at that time, and he had to rely on the Cuban president, Osvaldo Dorticós Torrado, for advice. Both leaders agreed that attack by the United States was going to happen, and they needed to prepare in whatever way they could. On October 26, Castro sent a private message to Khrushchev asking that the Soviet Union respond with a nuclear first strike if the United States invaded Cuba.

An Exchange of Letters

President Kennedy responded to Khrushchev's message on October 25. He expressed grave disappointment that, despite promises to the contrary earlier that year, the Soviet Union had gone ahead and shipped nuclear weapons to Cuba. He went on to say, "I repeat my regret that these events should cause a deterioration in our relations. I hope that your Government will take the necessary action to permit a restoration of the earlier situation."

The chairman responded the next day in a message almost three thousand words in length. In it, he asked that the United States withdraw the quarantine and promise not to attack Cuba. One excerpt read, "We, for our part, will declare that our ships, bound for Cuba, will not carry any kind of armaments. You would declare that the United States will not invade Cuba with its forces and will not support any sort of forces which might intend to carry out an invasion of Cuba. Then the necessity for the presence of our military specialists in Cuba would disappear." Khrushchev followed up the next day in a message asking for the United States to withdraw its own missiles from Turkey, and in exchange, the Soviet Union would dismantle its missiles in Cuba.

The Tipping Point

With tensions mounting, both sides were on high alert, waiting for the other shoe to drop. This was when the Cuban Missile Crisis claimed its one and only victim.

Major Rudolf Anderson was flying a reconnaissance mission over Cuba. He knew it was a dangerous situation because his plane would appear on Soviet radar, and surface-to-air (SAM) missiles could easily pick him out of the sky. But Anderson loved his job. He loved to fly. He insisted on being chosen for the mission even though he wasn't scheduled to fly that day.

Major Ivan Gerchenov was in command at the Soviet SAM site, and he was on edge, along with every Soviet soldier under his command. There were rumors that American paratroopers would be flown in to initiate an attack on a nearby town. There were lots of dots on his radar screen,

Major Rudolph Anderson's plane was shot down while on a reconnaissance mission over Cuba. His death helped to bring the Cuban Missile Crisis to a peaceful resolution.

but one in particular caught his attention, and Gerchenov ordered the gunners in his command to aim at the target. Gerchenov could not order the attack on "Target Number 33." His orders came from Soviet military headquarters in El Chico. At 10:19 a.m. on October 27, 1962, the order to fire was given, and Major Anderson's plane was shot down. Anderson was killed instantly.

In Washington, the Oval Office was in chaos. The death of Major Anderson was possibly an act of war perpetrated by the Soviet Union, but President Kennedy knew that he had to find out the facts before he could respond with force. If this were a deliberate attack by the USSR, it was a big departure from Khrushchev's pleas for peaceful resolution.

Khrushchev was equally concerned. He had ordered his troops to respond with force only as an act of self-defense, so to discover that an unarmed plane had been shot down without provocation was alarming to him.

The Final Day

On October 28, 1962, the Soviet Union and the United States agreed to a peaceful resolution of the Cuban Missile Crisis. The United States would agree not to attack Cuba, and the Soviet Union would dismantle its missiles in Cuba. Attorney General Robert Kennedy delivered the message to the Soviet ambassador, Anatoly Dobrynin, personally. The United States would also agree to withdraw its missiles from Turkey, but this part of the bargain was not made public until a few decades later. The crisis was over.

This haunting image is one of the last photos taken of President Kennedy before his assassination in Dallas, Texas.

CHAPTER THREE

The Faces of the Cold War

As we look at the events of the Cuban Missile Crisis and Bay of Pigs invasion, we often skip over discussing the broader historical significance of the key players. Some came from great political careers. Some went on to play a greater role in global politics. And some lived tragically short lives. Let's take a look at the historical figures who influenced and were influenced by this history-making moment in time.

John F. Kennedy

When we look at John F. Kennedy from a historical standpoint, his life and career are often overshadowed by his untimely death. On November 22, 1963, Kennedy was assassinated as he traveled in a motorcade through downtown Dallas, Texas. But to really understand his significance, let's take a look at his life.

John F. Kennedy was born May 29, 1917, one of the nine children of Joseph P. Kennedy, Sr. and Rose Fitzgerald Kennedy. Jack, as they called him, was not a healthy baby. As a child, he suffered from whooping cough, measles, and scarlet fever. He was never fully healthy for the remainder of his life, always suffering from an ailment of some sort, including a back injury that he sustained playing college football that would afflict him for the rest of his life. But he was always destined for greatness. It was Jack's father who announced that his son would end up being the first Catholic president of the United States. Jack himself, at the time attending Harvard, was not terribly sure of his father's plans for him. It wasn't until 1937, when Joe Kennedy, Sr. was appointed ambassador to England, that Jack became interested in politics.

During World War II, Jack joined the Navy. He was made commander of a patrol torpedo boat, the PT-109, and oversaw a crew of twelve men. Their job was to intercept Japanese ships trying to deliver supplies. One night, while the crew was patrolling the waters, a Japanese warship suddenly came into view, heading straight for their smaller boat. Lieutenant Kennedy was at the wheel and tried to swerve, but the warship smashed into the PT-109, splitting it in half and killing two of the crewmembers instantly. Kennedy reinjured his back in the crash, but he managed to gather his remaining crewmembers together and keep them alive as he led them to a nearby island where they were later rescued. For this, he was awarded the Navy and Marine Corps Medal.

When the war ended, Kennedy was still reeling from the death of his older brother, Joe, a Navy pilot who had been killed during a dangerous mission during the war. He decided he wanted to make a difference in the world, and this spurred him to run for Congress in Massachusetts's eleventh congressional district in 1946. He won, and over the next seven years, he served three terms in the House of Representatives and was elected to the United States Senate. He was only thirty-six. He knew his next step would be the presidency. In 1960, his father's prediction came true, and John F. Kennedy was elected president, the first Catholic and the youngest ever to be elected to the office. He was forty-three.

Kennedy's top priority as he assumed the presidency was foreign affairs. The United States and Soviet relations were at the top of his list, along with thwarting the spread of Communism.

The Peace Corps

The focus of the Peace Corps today is on education, particularly of women and girls across the globe, treatment of disease and hunger, and AIDS relief. But when it was established by executive order on March 1, 1961, by President Kennedy himself, the ultimate goal was to stop the spread of Communism through global outreach. The Soviet Union had hundreds of teachers, scientists, doctors, and nurses working globally in the service of their nation. The United States had no such program to help spread democracy. The African nations of Tanganyika and Ghana were the first countries to participate in the Peace Corps program. By the year 2000, one hundred thirty-five countries would find aid through the efforts of Peace Corps volunteers.

Alliance for Progress

During his presidency, Kennedy also sought to establish better relations with Latin America. Previous administrations had supported military dictatorships in Peru, Paraguay, Venezuela, and Cuba. But the people of those nations were suffering and angry. Through the Alliance for Progress, established in 1961, the United States would loan more than twenty billion dollars to Latin American nations to help promote democracy and social reform as well as allow for more citizens to own and control the use of land. Unfortunately, the plan ran into several obstacles. American businesses with interests in Latin America were more focused on their own prosperity than on social and political reform in those nations. Some Alliance funds were used to create counterinsurgency programs and train forces to help fight Communism in Latin America. Some wealthier Latin Americans fought against any kind of reform that could potentially damage their interests. So although the Alliance did help with the construction of housing, schools, airports, and hospitals, and with the distribution of free textbooks to students, the plan was considered a failure by the 1970s.

The Civil Rights Movement

During the 1960 election that would put President Kennedy into office, African American citizens were struggling to vote, despite the passage of the Fifteenth Amendment almost

The March on Washington on August 28, 1963, was attended by more than 200,000 civil rights protestors. It was at this march that Dr. Martin Luther King, Jr. delivered his "I Have a Dream" speech.

ninety years before, which allowed African American men the right to vote. (African American women gained the right with the passage of the Nineteenth Amendment in 1920.) But in several Southern states, many whites in positions of authority were using bullying tactics to keep African Americans from the polls. Throughout the United States, African Americans were facing extreme discrimination in schools, employment, and housing. The "Jim Crow" laws—a group of state and local laws that established a harsher set of rules for African American citizens—had been promoting segregation since the 1880s. The Civil Rights Movement sought to establish equality and end segregation once and for all. Although President Kennedy's support of the movement remains controversial to this day, he did push for civil rights legislation. Unfortunately, he did not live to see the passage of the Civil Rights Act, in 1964.

The Legacy of John F. Kennedy

The Kennedy presidency lasted less than three years, and yet many see him as one of the great presidents in United States history. Kennedy was responsible for a great many triumphs, but he also had his share of failures. According to a *Forbes* article from 2013, his looks and charm were an asset in an era when television was becoming the most relied-upon resource for news. Kennedy was the first president to appear in live, televised press conferences. This helped American citizens feel closer and more in touch with the White House and the man who represented it. Kennedy was young and a war hero. Many saw him as a beacon of progress and change to a nation still reeling from the Second World War and facing the spread of Communism. Further, his death was so sudden and so tragic that it crossed party lines, bringing a nation together as people mourned his loss.

Nikita Khrushchev

Many Americans know Nikita Khrushchev, Soviet premier, only for his involvement in the Cuban Missile Crisis and the ongoing Cold War relations with the United States. But there was a lot more to his rise to power and rule of the USSR.

Nikita Khrushchev was born in Kalinovka, a small Russian village, in 1894. When he joined the Bolsheviks in 1918, at the age of twenty-four, he was a firm believer in the workers' state. He was ambitious and worked his way up the ranks of the Communist Party, eventually moving to Moscow. Khrushchev helped mobilize troops to fight Nazi Germany during World War II, and by the time Joseph Stalin died in 1953, he was considered one of his most likely successors. He took over as premier of the USSR in 1957.

One of his first acts as premier was to distance himself from his predecessor, who made a practice of having any political opponents arrested and deported or executed. His address to denounce Joseph Stalin was given in 1956 and was known as the "secret speech." But because of Khrushchev's boisterous personality, the speech didn't stay secret for long, which created a great deal of tension in the USSR. Still, he traveled to Yugoslavia to apologize to Marshal Josip Broz Tito for events that had damaged relations between the two countries under Stalin's rule. Although Khrushchev still worked hard to stamp out opposition, he did try to

In Kennedy's Words

President John F. Kennedy was a "highly quotable" speaker. People still reference his famous quote, "ask not what your country can do for you—ask what you can do for your country" as part of one of the greatest inaugural addresses of the twentieth century. Let's take a look at some of his other quotable moments.

From Kennedy's televised address to the nation on the evening of October 22, 1962:

Many times in the past, the Cuban people have risen to throw out tyrants who destroyed their liberty. And I have no doubt that most Cubans today look forward to the time when they will be truly free—free from foreign domination, free to choose their own leaders, free to select their own system, free to own their own land, free to speak and write and worship without fear or degradation. And then shall Cuba be welcomed back to the society of free nations and to the associations of this hemisphere.

From a 1962 special address to Congress on the nation's health care needs:

> For one true measure of a nation is its success in fulfilling the promise of a better life for each of its members. Let this be the measure of our nation.

From a 1963 address to the UN General Assembly:

> Never before has man had such capacity to control his own environment, to end thirst and hunger, to conquer poverty and disease, to banish illiteracy and massive human misery. We have the power to make this the best generation of mankind in the history of the world—or make it the last.

Kennedy and Khrushchev met in Vienna in 1961, a year before the Cuban Missile Crisis. The mood at the meeting was tense, despite the smiles here.

help improve living standards for his country's citizens and reduced the power of the secret police that had come to be a feared entity during Stalin's regime. He released many political prisoners and even lowered control over censorship of the arts. Khrushchev also kicked off the space race when the USSR launched the satellite *Sputnik* into orbit in 1957.

Khrushchev preferred a peaceful coexistence with other capitalist nations, even visiting the United States in 1959. But he was a staunch believer in Communism. In 1961, he authorized the building of the Berlin Wall to keep West Germans out of East Germany, which was Communist, and to keep East Germans from crossing the border into the Federal Republic of Germany, a parliamentary democracy.

He also had an ongoing feud with fellow Communist, Mao Zedong, the leader of China. Mao opposed Khrushchev's peaceful coexistence approach to relations with capitalist countries and wanted a more aggressive military approach to help spread Communism across the globe. This disagreement and breakdown of relations between the USSR and China became known as the Sino-Soviet split. For American officials, this was now a "divide and conquer" situation and a huge turning point in the Cold War.

Unfortunately, not all Soviet officials were happy with the split from China or the outcome of the Cuban Missile Crisis. They saw continued food shortages across the USSR and Khrushchev's dominant behavior as a threat against the Soviet Union. In 1964, Soviet officials called for Khrushchev to resign as premier and the head of the Communist Party, and he did so without resistance. Khrushchev lived the rest of his life in peaceful retirement before succumbing to a heart attack in 1971.

The Legacy of Nikita Khrushchev

Nikita Khrushchev was considered by many to be an uneducated peasant who had inexplicably risen to power. He was loud and boisterous and often prone to outbursts. During a debate at the United Nations in 1960, he got everyone's attention by taking off his shoe and pounding it on the table. But Khrushchev wanted, and worked for, peace with the United States. He was a masterful negotiator. And many of his policies were enacted to help improve life for Soviet citizens after Stalin's death. Almost half a century after his death, historians still debate whether his many triumphs and failures add up to a capable leader.

Fidel Castro

Fidel Castro was one of the longest-serving, nonroyal, political leaders in modern history. The leader of the Communist revolution in Cuba, Castro was named premier of Cuba in 1959 after the overthrow of General Fulgencio Batista. This would make Cuba the first Communist nation in the Western Hemisphere, creating a tense situation with the United States.

Castro was born in 1926, the illegitimate son of a sugarcane farmer and a domestic servant who worked for his father's family. At that time, being born out of wedlock brought its own set of complications to a child's life, but Castro worked hard. He loved school, and he loved sports,

The Death of a Pilot

Major Rudolf Anderson wasn't scheduled to fly on October 27, 1962 (the twelfth day of the Cuban Missile Crisis), but when he heard about the mission, part of the ongoing "Operation Brass Knob," he insisted on getting the assignment.

The flight was to last one hour and fifteen minutes. Anderson's mission was to fly over the eastern part of Cuba to check out military deployments around the Guantanamo naval base and to investigate the Soviet military defense system.

Anderson knew the mission would be dangerous. From an altitude of 72,000 feet (21,946 meters), he would be an easy target for missiles, but he took his job seriously. It was 9:09 a.m. when Anderson's plane took off.

Around 10:19 a.m., a Soviet missile exploded near Anderson's plane, piercing the cockpit and likely killing him instantly. Upon hearing the news, President Kennedy remarked, "We are now in an entirely new ball game," according to an account published on History.com. United States military leaders urged Kennedy to launch airstrikes against Cuba, but Kennedy was not so sure that was the right move. It was possible, he surmised, that the missile launch was not authorized by Khrushchev himself. If that was the case, there was still a chance for diplomacy between the two nations. Khrushchev saw the situation spiraling out of control on his end as well. The next day, the Soviet ambassador Anatoly Dobrynin and Robert Kennedy met to discuss a peaceful resolution. Anderson's death marked the only combat death of the Cuban Missile Crisis.

especially baseball, but he was particularly interested in the fight for human rights.

By the time he entered the University of Havana to study law in 1945, Castro was an active participant in several student protests on campus. As time went by, his activism often took him out of Cuba. Castro took part in a failed attempt to overthrow dictator Rafael Trujillo, the ruler of the Dominican Republic at the time, and 1948 found him in Colombia, taking part in a riot after the assassination of Jorge Eliécer Gaitán Ayala, one of the leaders of Colombia's Liberal Party. The riot resulted in the deaths of thousands of people, but Castro and his friends were not charged with any crimes for their involvement.

Back in Cuba, Batista was slowly returning to power. He had served as president of Cuba from 1940 to 1944, but in the time since he had left office, the Cuban government had slowly begun to lose control. In 1950, Castro had graduated from college and opened a law office. He was eyeing a career in politics, so he ran for election to the Cuban House of Representatives. However, in 1952, the Cuban government fell, and Batista regained power, canceling the election. Many Cubans were grateful for the change in power, but many, including Castro, could see trouble on the horizon.

Batista was a tyrant. He imprisoned people who threatened his authority, took complete control of the university, press, and Congress, and embezzled money from the Cuban government. The "presidential elections" that took place in 1954 and 1958 were a total sham because Batista was the only candidate.

Castro was not sitting idly by during Batista's reign, however. He and several others who supported a revolution in Cuba had formed a group they called the "Movement." In 1953, this group, led by Castro, attacked an army barracks in Santiago de Cuba. But the attack was a failure, and Castro and his supporters, including his brother Raúl, were captured and imprisoned. Castro was sentenced to fifteen years in prison, but he was released in 1955 through a deal made with Batista's government.

During his time in prison, Fidel Castro had continued to plan for revolution, keeping up with supporters through letter writing. When Castro was released, he and Raúl left

Fidel Castro (*at far left*) marches in a parade in Havana in 1959. Che Guevara can be seen at right center.

for Mexico where they could continue to plan. In Mexico, Castro met Ernesto "Che" Guevara for the first time. Guevara believed that violent revolution against oppressive Latin American governments was the key to helping the poor in those countries. He was eager to join Castro's Movement.

Finally, in 1956, the Movement was prepared for revolution. Castro traveled back to Cuba with around eighty insurgents and plenty of weapons and prepared for attack in the city of Manzanillo. But Batista's army was more than prepared for the attack and killed or captured the majority of Castro's forces. Castro, Raúl, Guevara, and a group of their supporters escaped into the Sierra Maestra Mountains. From there, over the next two years, they carefully orchestrated guerrilla attacks against Batista's army that slowly began to weaken the government's hold.

In 1959, Batista fled to the Dominican Republic. Castro was thirty-two when he successfully overthrew the Cuban government. That year, he was made prime minister of Cuba, but it wasn't until 1961 that Castro declared publicly that he was a socialist. Cuba was a still a young nation that needed economic and military support, and it began to rely on the Soviet Union for the help it needed. This relationship with the USSR, in addition to Castro's policies that were put in place to help release the hold the United States had over Cuba, only served to break down Cuba's relationship with the United States. This breakdown put the United States government into crisis mode, and they began to formulate a plan to overthrow Castro and his Communist policies. But Castro was not deterred. The Bay of Pigs invasion by the United States and Operation Mongoose were both failures, and the so-called Cuban Missile Crisis, while peacefully resolved, did nothing to improve relations. In February 1962, John F. Kennedy declared a trade embargo on Cuba.

The Highs and Lows of the Castro Regime

Because of the trade embargo with the United States, the Cuban people in the 1960s had to learn to live life differently. They could no longer get cars or televisions or any other modern technology through trade with the United States. Food imports were now severely limited. Furthermore, Cuba

Trade embargoes with the United States led to food shortages across Cuba. Here, Cubans line up for bread before the meager supply runs out for the day.

struggled to find allies after the fall of the Soviet Union in 1991. The Soviet Union provided much of Cuba's oil in exchange for sugar and other crops. Without trade with the Soviet Union, the economy of Cuba suffered. Even today in Cuba people struggle to find food staples that are readily available in the United States, like meat, eggs, and milk.

Many Cuban people felt, and continue to feel today, that their freedoms were limited under socialist rule. Cuba has one political party, and there hasn't been a government-wide election since the 1960s. Castro also abolished freedom of the press by shutting down any newspapers that opposed him and abolished private business ownership. Because of the dire circumstances for many Cuban citizens, many of them—thousands every year—have risked their lives to cross the Straits of Florida in order to find political asylum in the United States and eventually apply for United States citizenship under the Cuban Adjustment Act.

To Castro's credit, during his rule, he did work hard to abolish legal discrimination. He helped build schools and hospitals, and he brought electricity to parts of Cuba that had previously been without.

Thawing Relations in the Twenty-First Century

Castro had emergency intestinal surgery in 2006, and during his recovery, he handed the reins of Cuba over to his brother, Raúl. In 2008, his health still delicate, Castro made the transition of power permanent. He passed away in 2016 after several years of staying out of the public eye. Relations between Cuba and the United States have been slowly thawing in the twenty-first century.

There is a growing Cuban American population in the United States, increasing to more than two million in 2015, which some say might account for increased tolerance. In 2014, President Barack Obama was the first president in decades to travel to Cuba with hopes of establishing better relations with the country. In 2015, the Cuban embassy reopened in Washington, DC, and the United States embassy reopened in Cuba. Early in 2016, direct mail flights between the United States and Cuba resumed. The restrictions on imports and exports between the two nations have expanded, now allowing some trade between the countries.

Robert F. Kennedy

Robert F. Kennedy was born November 20, 1925, the seventh of the nine children of Joseph Kennedy, Sr. and his wife, Rose. Like his older brother, Robert graduated from Harvard University. He then studied law at the University of Virginia. In 1951, having freshly graduated with his law degree, Robert Kennedy went to work as a lawyer for the United States Department of Justice. A year later, he managed his brother's campaign for the United States Senate. In 1959, he managed his brother's campaign again—this time, for the presidency. After the election, John F. Kennedy appointed his brother United States attorney general.

As attorney general, Robert Kennedy waged a war against organized crime and fought hard for civil rights. In a speech at the University of Georgia Law School, Kennedy said of the Supreme Court ruling for desegregation of schools, "I happen to believe that the 1954 decision was right. But my

Robert Kennedy is shown campaigning in Indiana during his 1968 run for the presidency. The day after he won the California primary, Kennedy was murdered.

belief does not matter. It is the law. Some of you may believe the decision was wrong. That does not matter. It is the law."

John F. Kennedy considered his younger brother to be one of his top advisors, particularly on the issue of relations with Cuba and the USSR, viewed by many as an unorthodox choice since he was attorney general and not Secretary of State. The younger Kennedy was at his brother's side throughout the failure of the Bay of Pigs invasion and the peaceful resolution of the Cuban Missile Crisis. After President Kennedy's death in 1963, Robert Kennedy resigned as attorney general and ran for Senate in 1964. As a New York senator, Kennedy worked hard to address the needs of the poor and underprivileged in his state. He also stood up for human rights overseas, and, after some consideration of the issues, spoke out against the war in Vietnam. In 1968, Robert Kennedy announced his own campaign for the presidency. However, just a few months later, only a day after winning the California primary, Kennedy was shot by an assassin named Sirhan Sirhan and died the next day. He was only forty-two.

The Legacy of Robert F. Kennedy

Robert Kennedy was a beloved champion of human rights throughout his political career. In 1968, shortly after his death, his widow, Ethel, established the Robert F. Kennedy Center for Justice and Human Rights. The organization works to keep Kennedy's dreams of worldwide social justice alive.

This painting shows George Washington and Marquis de Lafayette (*right*) on horseback at Valley Forge.

WASHINGTON AND LAFAYETTE AT VALLEY FORGE. COPYRIGHT, 1907.

CHAPTER FOUR

Negotiation and Innovation

The long history of diplomacy in the United States started before the American colonies became an independent nation. Before and during the Revolutionary War, the colonies negotiated for military aid from France. Benjamin Franklin and other members of the Secret Committee of Correspondence (eventually renamed the Committee for Foreign Affairs), wrote to contacts in Europe who they thought might be able to rally support for the American cause. They were successful, and the American colonies signed the **Treaty** of Alliance and Treaty of Amity and Commerce with France on February 6, 1778. Without the support of their French allies, the American forces likely would have fallen to the more powerful British army. When the revolution was over, the newly-formed United States government established the State Department, which would help the president handle foreign affairs and diplomacy with nations across the globe. The State Department continues to do so to this day.

Diplomacy is basically the art of negotiation between two nations. It helps to maintain peace and resolve conflicts without stirring up any additional hostility. Diplomacy is complicated and difficult, and if and when it fails, a war might be the result.

Diplomacy and the Cuban Missile Crisis

What made the Cuban Missile Crisis unique in the history of United States diplomacy was that talks with the Soviet Union were, in part, handled publicly by the United States president and the premier of the USSR themselves, with the secretary of state and other members of the cabinet acting as an advisory board to the president. This exchange has been described by many historians as a "high-stakes game of poker"—and for good reason. With both nations possessing nuclear weapons, the stakes were high. Relations between the Soviet Union and United States were already rocky. Kennedy and Khrushchev had met only once before, at the Summit Conference in Vienna in June 1961, and things had not gone well. The summit had seen the much-younger president get verbally pummeled by the premier. Kennedy told *Time* magazine's White House correspondent at the time, Hugh Sigey, "I never met a man like this. [I] talked about how a nuclear exchange would kill 70 million people in 10 minutes, and he just looked at me as if to say, 'So what?'" This exchange, the building of the Berlin Wall, and the Cold War as a whole created a unique situation that required quick thinking and immediate action.

But that wasn't the whole story. Outwardly, the American public saw Kennedy and Khrushchev go toe-to-toe, with the threat of nuclear strike on the horizon. But early in the process, the president made the decision to push for diplomacy, rather than preemptive strike or an invasion of Cuba. And rather than relying on the secretary of state, Kennedy placed the United States attorney general, his brother Robert, in charge of handling much of the diplomatic relations with the Soviet Union on his behalf. This was unheard of at the time. Robert Kennedy's job dipped into what is called "backdoor diplomacy," in which additional arrangements are made outside of the public eye and sometimes without public knowledge. Once John F. Kennedy announced the "quarantine" of Cuba, the Soviet and United States governments were in contact almost immediately, and this communication didn't cease until both sides followed through on their promises.

At the end of the Cuban Missile Crisis, Khrushchev agreed to remove Soviet nuclear missiles out of Cuba if the United States agreed not to invade Cuba. The one part of that compromise that the American public wasn't aware of for another twenty-five years was the agreement for the United States to remove its nuclear missiles from Turkey. Robert Kennedy met in secret with Soviet ambassador Anatoly Dobrynin to come to that agreement, acting on behalf of the United States president.

Backdoor Diplomacy Today

Backdoor diplomacy is nothing new to the United States government and continues to be used to this day, and this is particularly relevant in modern-day Russia. Just because the Cold War is over doesn't mean that relations between Russia and the United States have been completely healed. According to an article from *Bloomberg*, President Barack Obama relied on secret diplomacy to help resolve some of the conflict stemming from the Ukrainian revolution with Russia and its leader, Vladimir Putin. Since 2014, Russian forces have been in Ukraine, slowly annexing parts of it by force, using the instability of the Ukrainian government as

During the second half of the Obama administration, relations between the United States and Russia were aided by the strong diplomatic relationship between John Kerry and Sergei Lavrov.

leverage to do so. Rather than sending forces to Ukraine and potentially escalating the crisis, President Obama relied on Secretary of State John Kerry to maintain a flow of communication with Moscow.

Kerry had a diplomatic relationship with Russian foreign minister Sergei Lavrov. The two spoke on the phone frequently and met in person, sometimes without their staff members. So while Obama's relationship with Putin remained contentious, John Kerry continued to work with Lavrov to keep peace between the Russian and United States governments. Sometimes diplomacy represents evolution—rather than revolution—a course of slow progress, often taking years to work through a disagreement. Even at the end of the Cuban Missile Crisis, the United States and Soviet Union kept up the Cold War for the next thirty years.

Technology and the Cuban Missile Crisis

Technology also played an enormous role in the resolution of the Cuban Missile Crisis. Throughout the Cold War, the United States rushed to match the Soviet Union on space exploration and weaponry, while the Soviet Union did the same. Technology both led to and helped resolve the Cuban Missile Crisis and other key moments of the Cold War. Let's take a look at the role of technology during the early 1960s.

Weapons Technology

In 1955, Albert Einstein, Bertrand Russell, and other top scientists issued a manifesto calling for an end to nuclear

The Controversial Diplomacy of Henry Kissinger

In 1957, Harvard professor Henry Kissinger published his book *Nuclear Weapons and Foreign Policy*, which spoke out against the way that then-president Dwight Eisenhower handled aggression by the Soviet Union. Eisenhower and John Foster Dulles, his secretary of state, had worked against the spread of Communism by wielding the threat of massive retaliation with nuclear weapons. Kissinger advocated a more strategic and "flexible" approach that combined tactical nuclear weapons, conventional force, and development of new weapons technology. President Kennedy adopted this approach upon taking office and frequently asked Kissinger to consult on foreign policy. President Lyndon B. Johnson relied on Kissinger as well. During the first Nixon administration, Kissinger was made national security advisor.

Kissinger's tactics were unconventional. He and President Nixon preferred "backdoor diplomacy" and secrecy. They sought to establish a balance of power with the Soviet Union, a policy known as détente, rather than open rivalry. Kissinger reached out to North Vietnam, hoping to find an end to the Vietnam War. He won the Nobel Peace Prize for his efforts in 1973. That same year, he became secretary of state for Nixon's second term. But not everyone was pleased with Kissinger's tactics. Kissinger's "peace with honor" strategy to ending the war in Vietnam extended an already deadly and unpopular war by four years. He also initiated the bombing of Cambodia, killing between fifty thousand and one hundred fifty thousand Cambodian people, in an attempt to cut off supply lines to North Vietnam. A weakened Cambodia fell to Communism under the Khmer Rouge in 1975. Kissinger left office in 1977, but he continues to comment about foreign policy.

war. In the United Kingdom in 1958, the Campaign for Nuclear **Disarmament** was formed. This pushback against nuclear weapons led to a moratorium on nuclear testing in the United States and the United Kingdom as well as a global ban on testing nuclear weapons in Antarctica. But by 1961, Nikita Khrushchev was restless.

He had promised President Kennedy in June of that year that the Soviet Union wouldn't test any more nuclear weapons if the United States also refrained from testing weapons. But he wanted to show off the military might of the Soviet Union. The only problem was that he didn't have a bomb anywhere near big enough. Therefore, between July and October, 1961, Khrushchev ordered the construction of the Tsar Bomba (also known as Big Ivan). The Tsar Bomba weighed 27 tons (24 metric tons), almost as much as the plane that would carry it. On October 30, the Soviet Union dropped the bomb over the Mityushikha Bay testing range. The resulting explosion was 1,400 times more powerful than the bombs dropped on Hiroshima and Nagasaki combined. The mushroom cloud created by Tsar Bomba was 210,000 feet tall (64,000 meters).

During John F. Kennedy's presidential campaign, he referred to a "missile gap" in the United States. This "gap" implied that the United States had fallen behind the Soviet Union in creation of nuclear missiles. He said in a speech, "We are moving into a period when the Soviet Union will be outproducing us two or three to one in the field of missiles—a period relatively vulnerable and when our retaliatory force will be in danger of destruction through a Soviet surprise attack—the period of the missile gap."

Tsar Bomba remains the largest, most destructive nuclear weapon to have ever been detonated. Luckily, at the time of detonation, it was only being tested, and no one was harmed.

The Soviet Union had succeeded in building the first **intercontinental ballistic missile** (ICBM)—a missile with the ability to travel upwards of 4,000 miles (6,437 kilometers) to hit a target. (This missile was even used to help launch *Sputnik*.) By 1959, the United States also had an ICBM, called the Atlas. The assumption by Kennedy's campaign and the American media is that the Soviet Union had used the years between 1957 and 1959 to stockpile as many ICBMs as possible while the United States still worked to develop an ICBM of their own. But in reality, the USSR had only around ten intercontinental ballistic missiles total. The United States had fifty-seven.

Flight and Surveillance Technology

The Central Intelligence Agency (CIA) was formed in 1947 by President Harry S. Truman. The role of the agency was to coordinate United States intelligence activities, including collecting and evaluating information that could potentially affect national security. And over the next ten years, the CIA worked to develop a system for "overhead reconnaissance," or photographs secretly taken from above. (This type of intelligence is referred to as "**imagery intelligence**," or by its acronym, IMNIT.) At the time, the focus of this need was on the Soviet Union, and Soviets were becoming increasingly protective of their borders. Airplanes like the Boeing RB-47 were sent on reconnaissance missions but risked being shot down or being unable to get near a target. For this reason, the **U-2** spy plane was developed.

The U-2 Dragon Lady could carry up to seven hundred pounds (318 kilograms) of equipment at an altitude of seventy thousand feet (21,336 meters), or about thirteen miles (21 kilometers) in the air. (For comparison, a commercial airplane cannot, by law, fly higher than forty-five thousand feet.) It was a U-2 mission that provided the images of missile sites in Cuba for President Kennedy, and Major Rudolf Anderson was flying the same type of plane on his fateful reconnaissance mission to Cuba at the pinnacle of the Cuban Missile Crisis. The U-2 is still used to this day, since satellite

Hedy Lamarr and the Cuban Missile Crisis

Hedy Lamarr was consistently labeled "the most beautiful woman in the world" throughout her life. The star of such films as *Samson and Delilah*, *Ziegfeld Girl*, and *Algiers* was born in Austria in 1914 and escaped a marriage to an Austrian weapons manufacturer by immigrating to the United States before World War II.

Hedy Lamarr is primarily known for being an actress, but she was also a brilliant mathematician and inventor.

But while Lamarr's claim to fame was acting, she was also a brilliant inventor and mathematical genius. And we are still benefitting from her most famous invention today.

Lamarr came up with the idea of a frequency-hopping wireless signal that could be used to guide torpedoes toward their targets. The idea was that a wireless radio signal would switch among multiple frequency channels so that enemies would not be able to jam the signal. To help realize her idea, Lamarr brought in George Antheil. Antheil was a musician and an inventor, so he came up with a concept similar to the rolls used in player pianos, allowing for switching among eighty-eight channels. The idea was patented in 1942, but the United States Navy wanted no part of it at the time. Lamarr's efforts to help the United States fight the Germans were rebuffed, and she was told to go back to Hollywood and use her star power to sell war bonds. (She raised seven million dollars).

But the invention did not stay on the shelf for long. During the Cuban Missile Crisis, the navy used jamming-proof technology on their ships for the very first time, enabling the ship to communicate with the torpedo wirelessly and without the signal being jammed.

Frequency-hopping spread spectrum (FHSS) technology was finally declassified by the government in the 1980s, and today the technology is used in modern cellphones. Lamarr was not officially honored for her work until 1997.

The U-2 spy plane was one of the most important innovations of the twentieth century.

technology might find a satellite on the wrong side of the planet when **surveillance** is needed, and drones have not developed to the point in which they can carry the same payload or fly at the same altitude as the U-2. Of course, upgrades have been made to the U-2 in the past sixty years. Modern U-2s have better engines, computerized cockpit equipment, and upgraded photographic equipment—digital photography is used now, rather than film.

Additional Developments

During Operation Mongoose, the United States came up with a variety of plots that could potentially be used to remove Fidel Castro from power. Some of them seemed right out of a James Bond film, and some were just strange. But all required innovation in the fields of technology and science. One plan, for instance, called for an exploding seashell. Since Castro was a fan of scuba diving and had some usual places he loved to visit to do so, the idea was that the CIA would place a shell so beautiful that Castro would have to pick it up during one of this dives. The booby-trapped shell would explode, killing him instantly. Unfortunately, this technological advancement did not make it past CIA head of Cuban operations Desmond Fitzgerald. (There was also a plot to present Castro with a poisoned diving suit.) Another plot involved "character assassination" that would lead not to Castro's death, but rather to his humiliation. An operative would wait for Castro to put his shoes out to be shined while he was traveling and then dust Castro's shoes with thallium salts, a depilatory, which would cause his beard to fall out.

Innovation was key during the Cold War, whether it was through technological means or diplomatic ones. And no matter if the idea was outlandish or brilliant, each had something to contribute to the effort.

United States president George Bush and Soviet president Mikhail Gorbachev declared an end to the Cold War on December 3, 1989.

CHAPTER FIVE

The Legacy of the Bay of Pigs and the Cuban Missile Crisis

The Soviet Union of 1991 was made up of fifteen republics: Ukraine, the Russian Federation, Belarus, Armenia, Azerbaijan, Kazakhstan, Kyrgyzstan, Moldova, Turkmenistan, Tajikistan, Uzbekistan, Georgia, Latvia, Lithuania, and Estonia. But the Republic was on very shaky ground.

The Soviet people were unhappy. Since assuming the leadership of the USSR in 1985, President Mikhail Gorbachev had been struggling to correct a lot of wrongs perpetrated by earlier leadership. Joseph Stalin, during his reign, had called for absolute loyalty of every citizen. People were not allowed to protest. **Dissenters** were executed or arrested. Gorbachev sought to correct that wrongdoing by introducing some new policies. The first of these was known as **glasnost**. Its goal was to completely eliminate any remaining Stalinist oppression. There would no longer be banned books or secret police. Newspapers were to be allowed, once again, to speak out against the government. Other political parties were allowed to participate in elections.

Perestroika, the second set of reforms that Gorbachev put forth, would fix the Soviet economy by restructuring it and loosening some of the control the government had over businesses. This allowed people to own their own businesses for the first time since the 1920s. Unhappy workers were given the right to protest for better working conditions and pay. And trade with outside nations was once again encouraged.

These policy changes were a step in the right direction, but many Soviet people didn't see the changes happening fast enough and were unhappy. There were still food shortages as the economic renewal struggled to take off.

Gorbachev also vowed to reduce military influence in the Warsaw Pact nations of Eastern Europe: Albania, Bulgaria, Czechoslovakia, East Germany, Hungary, Poland, and Romania. He called for a withdrawal of troops from Afghanistan, where the USSR had been fighting a war since 1979.

The first revolution began in Poland in 1989. The Berlin Wall fell in November of that year. Then Czechoslovakia overthrew the Communist government of that nation. The spirit of independence grew. Other nations followed in breaking free from Soviet control. In 1991, Estonia, Lithuania, and Latvia—known collectively as the Baltic states—each declared their independence. The Soviet people began to see the possibility of independence on the horizon. Belarus, the Russian Federation, and Ukraine broke with the Soviet government in December 1991. Eight of the nine remaining republics followed suit within weeks. (Georgia would not declare its independence until a few years later.) The Soviet Union was no more. With the dissolution of the USSR came the end of the Cold War with the United States. One of the longest conflicts in American history, the Cold War spanned almost five decades, leaving behind a legacy of distrust that has been carried into the twenty-first century.

After the Crisis

The reality of the Cuban Missile Crisis and what it has become over fifty years later are quite different. Some historical retellings paint John F. Kennedy as a hero, a powerful politician whose skills and devotion to the United States carried the nation through the crisis with as little damage as possible. Kennedy was in favor of that version of the story. After the Bay of Pigs invasion and other failed operations to remove Fidel Castro from power, he needed a win, and this was a big one. But the reality was that the crisis was not contained within thirteen days.

Although the Cuban Missile Crisis had ended officially on October 28, it was months before each side followed through completely on their end of the compromise. The United States quarantine of Cuba remained in place until late November. It wasn't until several months later, in April, 1963, that the United States dismantled the nuclear missiles in Turkey. But the removal of the Soviet missiles in Cuba was a somewhat complicated matter that carried on until December, 1962.

Castro Reacts

Fidel Castro is frequently left out of the retelling of the Cuban Missile Crisis because he continued to pose a threat even after the United States and the Soviet Union had come to an agreement. Castro was angry with Khrushchev, his ally, for leaving him out of the negotiations between the United States and the Soviet Union.

He was also still on edge about the Bay of Pigs invasion and feared another attack. As a result, he insisted on keeping a number of the nuclear warheads that the Soviet Union had agreed to dismantle and remove from Cuba in case of another attack by the United States like the Bay of Pigs. (There were certain nuclear missiles that had been shipped in for that purpose months before, and the United States wasn't even aware of around one hundred of the missiles in question.) Fearing a strong reaction by Castro, Chairman Khrushchev sent in Soviet deputy prime minister Anastas Mikoyan to deal with Castro and keep him from doing anything rash. At last, in December 1962, Mikoyan, seeing that the Soviet Union was going to have a lot of trouble controlling its Cuban allies, convinced Castro that certain Soviet laws prohibited transferring ownership of the missiles to Cuba. On December 20, those missiles arrived back in the Soviet Union, and many say that this date was the true end of the Cuban Missile Crisis.

The Shape of the Cold War

Although the Cuban Missile Crisis represented the utmost of dangerous moments during the Cold War, it actually

Fidel Castro paid a visit to the Soviet Union in 1964. He is shown standing next to Soviet premier Nikita Khrushchev.

did a lot to help Soviet and United States relations. First, the USSR and United States agreed to establish a "hot line" communication link between their governments so that the two nations could better communicate should any future conflicts arise. Further, the USSR and the United States went on to sign the Limited Nuclear Test Ban Treaty

Pop Culture Legacy

In the years surrounding the Cuban Missile Crisis, Americans saw a rise in **pop culture** references to spies, intrigue, and the possibility of nuclear war.

Spy vs. Spy was a comic strip was created by Antonio Prohias. Prohias was born in Cuba, where he worked as a cartoonist. But his caricatures caught the eye of someone who was not impressed with his anti-Communist works of art: Fidel Castro. Prohias fled to the United States in 1960, where a year later his black and white feuding spies were picked up by *MAD* magazine. Although the Cold War has been over for decades, the spies still work hard to bring misfortune to each other.

In 1961, the Fantastic Four were introduced by Jack Kirby and Stan Lee: Dr. Reed Richards, Sue Storm, Johnny Storm, and Ben Grimm. In the first issue, the four are flying an experimental rocket into space in order to "beat the [Communists]." (The Soviet Union had launched its first manned flight into orbit that April.) Unlike some of the other superhero comics of the time, where battles were fought against euphemistic villains, the Fantastic Four went head-to-head with Communism itself.

A 1964 film, *Dr. Strangelove or: How I Learned to Stop Worrying and Love the Bomb*, was probably the greatest cultural reflection of the Cuban Missile Crisis. In this dark comedy, Brigadier General Jack D. Ripper believes that the fluoridation of the American water supply is a Communist plot and sets out to take down the USSR with America's Doomsday Machine, which has the ability to destroy life on earth. Meanwhile, the nation's top generals try to sort out the mess from the war room. None of them are really "sane" enough to have control over weapons of mass destruction. *Dr. Strangelove* is a comical reflection of power gone mad.

The film *Dr. Strangelove: or How I Learned to Stop Worrying and Love the Bomb* is a Cold War parody.

on July 25, 1963. This treaty suggested a huge change from Khrushchev's demeanor at the Summit Conference in Vienna on the subject of nuclear testing. The treaty prohibited nuclear explosions underwater, in the atmosphere, and in outer space. It allowed underground tests, provided that radioactive debris would not fall outside of the borders of the nation performing the test. It also put the Soviet Union and United States on the path toward complete disarmament, effectively ended the arms race, and called for no more environmental contamination by radioactive substances. In the United States, it took some convincing to assure the public and members of the Senate that the treaty was a good idea, especially with the recent memory of a brush with nuclear disaster. But the treaty was passed by the Senate and ratified that October. In 1968, the United States and the Soviet Union both signed the Treaty on the Non-Proliferation of Nuclear Weapons (NPT). This prevented the two superpowers from supplying nuclear technology to other countries. Although both the United States and Russia possess nuclear weapons to this day, work toward complete disarmament continues.

The United States and Russia Today

In early 1992, Russian president Boris Yeltsin made his first visit to the United States since the dissolution of the Soviet Union. Russia had taken over the Soviet Union's chair in the UN Security Council, and this was Yeltsin's first opportunity to attend on behalf of his country. President

George H.W. Bush and Yeltsin met several times during the visit, finally issuing a joint statement to let the world know that "Russia and the United States do not regard each other as potential adversaries." The countries continued to work toward peace through the late 1990s and early 2000s, even working together to launch the International Space

The relationship between Barack Obama and Vladimir Putin was tense during the Obama administration. Here, they interact at the 2016 G20 summit in China.

Station. But more recent conflicts have once again heightened tensions between the United States and Russia.

United States and Russian Conflicts

Syria has been engaged in a civil war since 2011, when protests against the Syrian government escalated into large-scale violence against the Syrian people. The conflict has given way to the rise of dangerous terrorist organizations

Russian airstrikes in Syria over the past several years caused masses of Syrians to flee the country.

within Syria, including ISIS (Islamic State in Iraq and Syria). As of 2015, eleven million people have been forced out of their homes and over 250,000 people have been killed. The United States government would like to see Syrian president Bashar al-Assad removed from power because of the violence he has perpetrated against the Syrian people. Russia has interests in Syria, including a port in Tartous that holds Russia's Black Sea fleet, and thus supports Assad and continues to supply the Syrian government with weapons. To keep ISIS and other terrorist organizations at bay, Russia began a series of airstrikes on the city of Aleppo, resulting in thousands of civilian casualties. Talks between the United States and Russia have thus far been unsuccessful.

The United States and Russia also continue to be engaged in conflict over Russia's annexation of Crimea and parts of Ukraine. Although Russia's takeover of Crimea occurred without violence, the situation remains tense as the United States government fears an outburst of violence in that region due to Russian aggression.

During the 2016 election between Hillary Clinton and Donald Trump, the United States government feared interference by Russian hackers might sway the vote. According to an article from the *Washington Post* on November 24, 2016, Russia might be responsible for weakening the Democratic Party in order to put the less-experienced candidate, Donald Trump, in office through spreading of propaganda, creating right-wing websites and social media accounts, and publicizing false information.

Ongoing disagreements between the United States and Russia continue to compromise any peace efforts made during

Many Cubans celebrated when the death of former Cuban dictator Fidel Castro was announced in November 2016.

The Legacy of the Bay of Pigs and the Cuban Missile Crisis

the years since the collapse of the Soviet Union. Many have said that the friction is at its highest level since the fall of the Berlin Wall, and only time and continued diplomacy can help to heal the relationship.

The United States and Cuba Today

After the Bay of Pigs invasion and the Cuban Missile Crisis, relations between the United States and Cuba were at a standstill for many years. The trade embargo remained in place, and after the fall of the Soviet Union—Cuba's biggest ally—the economy of Cuba continued to suffer. Since the embargo began, thousands of Cuban refugees have sought political asylum in the United States, risking their lives to travel to Florida by boat.

In the 1990s, the passage of the Helms-Burton Act added nations that traded with Cuba to the embargo after Cuba shot down two American planes over international waters, both carrying civilians. But in 2001, restrictions were relaxed in the wake of Hurricane Michelle when the United States agreed to sell food to Cuba. The United States remains the top supplier of food to Cuba.

While Cuba remains a Communist nation, relations with the United States continue to improve. Fidel Castro left office officially in 2008, leaving control of Cuba in the hands of his brother, Raúl, and the younger Castro is slowly warming to the idea of improving relations with the United States. Raúl Castro and President Barack Obama met in 2016. During that meeting, President Obama said, "I affirm that Cuba's destiny will not be decided by the

United States or any other nation." He went on to say, "Cuba is sovereign and rightly has great pride, and the future of Cuba will be decided by Cubans, not by anybody else." While the embargo remains in place, restrictions have been loosened somewhat, and the death of Fidel Castro in 2016 brought hope to a lot of Cuban people and refugees who had suffered under his rule.

After the Crisis

On November 2, 1962, President John F. Kennedy addressed the nation once again. His words, in part, spoke of hope for renewed relations with both the USSR and Cuba:

> *My fellow citizens, I want to take this opportunity to report on the conclusions which this Government has reached on the basis of yesterday's aerial photographs which will be made available tomorrow, as well as other indications, namely, that the Soviet missile bases in Cuba are being dismantled, their missiles and related equipment are being crated, and the fixed installations at these sites are being destroyed.*
>
> *The United States intends to follow closely the completion of this work through a variety of means, including aerial surveillance, until such time as an equally satisfactory international means of verification is effected.*
>
> *While the quarantine remains in effect, we are hopeful that adequate procedures can be developed for international inspection of Cuba-bound cargoes. The*

International Committee of the Red Cross, in our view, would be an appropriate agent in this matter.

The continuation of these measures in air and sea, until the threat to peace posed by these offensive weapons is gone, is in keeping with our pledge to secure their withdrawal or elimination from this hemisphere. It is in keeping with the resolution of the Organization of American States, and it is in keeping with the exchange of letters with Chairman Khrushchev of October 27th and 28th.

Progress is now being made toward the restoration of peace in the Caribbean, and it is our firm hope and purpose that this progress shall go forward.

Chronology

1867 The United States purchases Alaska from Russia.

1891 Americans begin providing aid during Russian famine.

1917 Bolsheviks, led by Vladimir Lenin, overthrow Nicholas II, ending centuries of czarist rule.

1922 The Union of Soviet Socialist Republics (USSR) is established.

1929 Joseph Stalin becomes the ruler of the USSR.

1945 World War II comes to an end.

1947 Communists seize power in Poland; President Truman announces Truman Doctrine, asking for the United States to provide aid to countries threatened by the USSR.

1949 The USSR tests its first atomic bomb.

1955 Nikita Khrushchev becomes the leader of the USSR after a long struggle for power with Georgy Malenkov following Stalin's death.

1959	Fidel Castro becomes premier of Cuba, instituting a Communist government.
1960	John F. Kennedy becomes president of the United States.
1961	The Bay of Pigs invasion of Cuba occurs; East Germany builds the Berlin Wall.
1962	The Cuban Missile Crisis takes place over a period of thirteen days.
1963	President John F. Kennedy is assassinated in Dallas, Texas; Lyndon B. Johnson is sworn in as president.
1964	Nikita Khrushchev is removed from office.
1989	The Berlin Wall comes down.
1991	The Soviet Union is abolished. Boris Yeltsin becomes president of Russia.
2014	President Barack Obama orders restoration of full diplomatic relations with Cuba.
2015	The Cuban embassy reopens in Washington, DC, and the United States embassy reopens in Cuba.
2016	Fidel Castro dies.

Glossary

Cold War The conflict between the United States and the USSR that lasted forty-five years.

Communism Political theory in which all property is owned by the public and distributed based on need.

czar The title given to a monarchial ruler of Russia between the sixteenth century and the Russian Revolution of 1917.

diplomacy The act of managing relations between nations through negotiation and peace-keeping efforts.

disarmament The act of reducing and eliminating the necessity for weapons within a nation.

dissenter An individual who openly opposes a decision or ideology.

embargo An official ban on trade or business with another nation.

espionage The act of spying or employing spies in order to obtain information about another nation.

fallout shelter An enclosed shelter designed to protect occupants from radioactivity, usually following a nuclear explosion.

glasnost A policy introduced by Mikhail Gorbachev that was meant to open up the Soviet government and allow for information to be exchanged more freely.

guerrilla An unconventional form of warfare that uses sabotage and other unexpected tactics in battle.

imagery intelligence Information and images gathered through aerial and satellite photography.

intercontinental ballistic missile (ICBM) A guided missile, capable of traveling over 3,400 miles (5,472 kilometers), that is designed to deliver a nuclear warhead to a predetermined location.

perestroika Government policy introduced by Mikhail Gorbachev in the Soviet Union during the 1980s that called for reforming and renewing the Soviet economy.

pop culture Popular trends, ideas, people, and perspectives that help to shape modern society.

premier Official title of a prime minister or other head of government, particularly in the Soviet Union after 1917.

revolution A sudden or very fast change in power within a nation, sometimes through force.

surveillance Close observation used to gather information about a criminal or spy.

treaty A signed agreement between two countries.

U-2 Spy plane developed in the 1950s that can fly at an altitude around seventy thousand feet, making aerial intelligence gathering easier and more efficient.

Bibliography

"The Bay of Pigs Invasion." Central Intelligence Agency, April 18, 2016. https://www.cia.gov/news-information/featured-story-archive/2016-featured-story-archive/the-bay-of-pigs-invasion.html.

Brinkley, Alan. "The Legacy of John F. Kennedy." *The Atlantic*, August 2013. http://www.theatlantic.com/magazine/archive/2013/08/the-legacy-of-john-f-kennedy/309499/.

"Cuba: What You Need to Know About the U.S. Embargo." United States Department of the Treasury, July 26, 2001. https://www.treasury.gov/resource-center/sanctions/Documents/tab4.pdf.

Dewey, Caitlin. "A Photographic Guide to the World's Embalmed Leaders." *The Washington Post*, March 8, 2013. https://www.washingtonpost.com/news/worldviews/wp/2013/03/08/a-photographic-guide-of-the-worlds-embalmed-leaders/.

Dobbs, Michael. *One Minute to Midnight*. New York: Alfred A. Knopf, 2008.

Holom, Brittany, Alyssa Haas, and Yury Barmin. "U.S.-Russia Relations Are at a Real Low. Here's the Diplomacy That Is Working." *The Washington Post*,

November 5, 2016. https://www.washingtonpost.com/news/monkey-cage/wp/2016/11/05/u-s-russia-relations-are-at-a-real-low-heres-the-diplomacy-that-is-working/.

Raab, Nathan. "Why John F. Kennedy's Legacy Endures 50 Years After His Assassination." *Forbes*, November 13, 2013. http://www.forbes.com/sites/nathanraab/2013/11/13/why-john-f-kennedys-legacy-endures-50-years-after-his-assassination/#73e10bad6e9d.

Smith, Samantha. "5 Facts About U.S. Relations with Cuba." Pew Research Center, March 18, 2016. http://www.pewresearch.org/fact-tank/2016/03/18/5-facts-about-u-s-relations-with-cuba/.

Suddath, Claire. "A Brief History of U.S. Cuba Relations." *Time*, April 15, 2009. http://content.time.com/time/nation/article/0,8599,1891359,00.html.

Thrall, Nathan, and Jesse James Wilkins. "Kennedy Talked, Khrushchev Triumphed." *New York Times*, May 22, 2008. http://www.nytimes.com/2008/05/22/opinion/22thrall.html.

Timberg, Craig. "Russian Propaganda Effort Helped Spread 'Fake News' During Election, Experts Say." *The Washington Post*, November 24, 2016. https://www.washingtonpost.com/business/economy/russian-propaganda-effort-helped-spread-fake-news-during-election-experts-say/2016/11/24/793903b6-8a40-4ca9-b712-716af66098fe_story.html.

Further Information

Books

Coleman, David. *The Fourteenth Day: JFK and the Aftermath of the Cuban Missile Crisis: Based on the Secret White House Tapes.* New York, NY: W.W. Norton & Company, 2013.

Douglass, James W. *JFK and the Unspeakable: Why He Died and Why It Matters.* New York, NY: Touchstone, 2010.

Kennedy, Robert F. *Thirteen Days: A Memoir of the Cuban Missile Crisis.* New York, NY: W.W. Norton & Company, 1999.

Rasenberger, Jim. *The Brilliant Disaster: JFK, Castro, and America's Doomed Invasion of Cuba's Bay of Pigs.* New York, NY: Scribner, 2012.

Websites

The Central Intelligence Agency
https://www.cia.gov/index.html
The CIA website includes a resource library with videos, reports, and other publications on espionage and many other topics.

The Cold War Museum

http://www.coldwar.org/

The Cold War Museum website features Cold War activities, including a trivia game.

John F. Kennedy Presidential Library and Museum

https://www.jfklibrary.org

The JFK website has interactive features that allow you to become immersed in the history of the Kennedy administration.

The White House Website

https://www.whitehouse.gov

The White House website offers various resources on foreign policy, in particular a timeline of diplomatic engagement regarding relations between the United States and Cuba.

Videos

JFK's Cuban Missile Crisis Speech

https://www.youtube.com/watch?v=EgdUgzAWcrw

This video shows President Kennedy's Cuban Missile Crisis speech on October 22, 1962.

The Tsar Bomba

https://www.youtube.com/watch?v=3eX3V-cL6gI

This video from the History Channel records the Tsar Bomba test drop on October 30, 1961.

Index

Page numbers in **boldface** are illustrations. Entries in **boldface** are glossary terms.

Alliance for Progress, 52
Anderson, Rudolf, 45–46, 61, 79
arms race, 6, 20, 92

backdoor diplomacy, 73–76
Batista, Fulgencio, 7, 23, 60, 62–64
Bay of Pigs invasion, 8–9, 30–37, 87–88, 98
Berlin Wall, 59, 86, 98
Bolsheviks, 13–14, 55
Bush, George H.W., 93

Campaign for Nuclear **Disarmament**, 77
Cardona, José Miró, 31
Castro, Fidel, 7–8, 22–26, 60, 99
  Bay of Pigs invasion and, 36–37
  Cuban Missile Crisis and, 43–44, 87–88
Central Intelligence Agency (CIA), 79
Civil Rights Movement, 52–54
Cold War, 5–6, 87, 88–92

technology and, 75–83
Communism, 7, 26, 51–52, 59
  fear of, 20–22
Communist Manifesto, The (Marx), 20
"containment" strategy, 20
Cuba, and USSR relationship, 27
Cuban Adjustment Act, 66
Cuban Missile Crisis, 9, 35, 39–47, 79, 81, 87, 98
  and diplomacy, 72
  Soviet and United States relations and, 88
czar, 11–14

diplomacy, 5, 9, 27, 41, 61–76, 98
disarmament, 77
dissenters, 85
Duma, 12–13

embargo, 26, 65, 98–99
Engels, Friedrich, 20
espionage, 34

fallout shelter, 6

glasnost, 85–86
Gorbachev, Mikhail, 85–86

110 The Bay of Pigs and the Cuban Missile Crisis

guerrilla, 32, 36, 64

Helms-Burton Act, 98
Hiroshima, 6, 18, 77
Hitler, Adolf, 15–16, 18

imagery intelligence, 79
intercontinental ballistic missile (ICBM), 78

Kennedy, Bobby, 38–39
Kennedy, John F., 29, 33, 39, 49–55, 56–57, 72–73, 87, 99–100
Kennedy, Robert F., 67–69, 73
Khrushchev, Nikita, 55–60, 72–73, 77
   Cuban Missile Crisis and, 43–44
Kissinger, Henry, 76

Lamarr, Hedy, 80–81
Latin America, 26, 52, 64
Lenin, Vladimir, 13, 14, 17
Limited Nuclear Test Ban Treaty, 89, 92

Marx, Karl, 20
McCarthy, Joseph, 24–25

Nagasaki, 6, 18, 77
negotiation, 9, 34–35, 42, 71–73
Nixon, Richard, 29–30
nuclear war, 6

Obama, Barack, 67, 74–75, 98–99

Operation Mongoose, 38–39, 82

Peace Corps, 51–52
perestroika, 86
pop culture, 90
premier, 8

revolution, 12–14, 17, 20, 60, 63, 64
Russia, 11–14

socialism, 13, 22
Sputnik, 59
Stalin, Joseph, 14–17, 55, 85
surveillance, 79–82

Taylor, Maxwell, 37
trade **embargo**, 26
Treaty of Alliance and Treaty of Amity and Commerce, 71
Treaty on the Non-Proliferation of Nuclear Weapons (NPT), 92
Tsar Bomba, 77

United States and Cuba relations, 98
United States and Russia conflicts, 94–98
United States and Russia relations, 92–94
U-2 spy plane, 79, 82

weapons technology, 75–79

Yeltsin, Boris, 92–93

About the Author

Bethany Bryan is a professional writer, copy editor, and editor. She enjoys studying and writing about history and visiting presidential museums. She has published books with Scholastic, Adams Media, and Rosen Publishing. Bethany lives in North Carolina.

WITHDRAWN